THE SUNSET
BEFORE DAWN

THERESA HODGE

This book is dedicated to Carmi H. and to every reader who supported me over the years.

BLURB

One Night.
A stranger.
Sweeps in like a hero.
The past and the future collide.
My heart remembers him the moment we meet. My
head does not. He's tall, charismatic, seductively
attractive, and before I know it I'm falling fast.
The harder I feel the more entranced I became.
What is it about this stranger that makes my body ache
as well as my heart?
The truth shatters me like a sudden storm...
Nothing in my life will ever be the same, after the sunset
before dawn.

ACKNOWLEDGMENTS

I would like to express many thanks to all the people who helped my manuscript shine. Thank you to my heavenly father, my family, book formatter, editor/proofreader, and book cover designer. Last but not least, to all of my readers who purchases and download my books.

CHAPTER ONE
ANNA

IT WAS the same dream I'd had over and over for as long as I can remember. I'm running through the woods in the dark of night. For some reason, I know where I'm going. I'm meeting someone, but I'm not sure who it is. All I know is I can sense him nearby. I come to a clearing in the woods lit by moonlight. I look down and I'm wearing a long black dress with a corset...something out of another time. I know he's near me... I can feel his breath on the back of my neck as he comes up behind, sending a shiver down my spine. My heart starts to race as his long fingers close around my arms. I close my eyes as he bends his head and kisses my neck. I let out a gasp as his hand closes over my chest, pulling down my dress and exposing my breasts to the cold night air. His hands reach up to cup me, playing with my nipples until they become hardened points.

I moan with pleasure as he slowly turns me around, and just as he bends down to kiss me–

Beep. Beep. Beep.

I let out a frustrated groan and hit the snooze button on my alarm, trying to go back to the very hot dream I was having. It was always the same...as soon as he'd turn me around and start to kiss me, I'd wake up. It was the biggest tease that my subconscious had ever played on me. I closed my eyes and imagined the woods, and the clearing, and the moonlight, and his kisses on my neck... it was no use. The dream was gone, and it was time for me to get up and get myself ready for the day.

I sat up and climbed out of my bed, walking over to the window. It was a gray, drizzly kind of day, and I wanted nothing more than to go back to sleep. But, I knew that wasn't an option. The only choice I had was to hop in the shower and start my morning routine if I wanted to make it to work on time .

Maybe it was a movie I saw, or a scene from a book I read. As I stood in the shower lathering myself up with body wash, I thought about why I kept having the same dream. It must be something I'd seen before, because it felt strangely familiar. And extremely arousing. Maybe the reason I kept having the dream was because I needed to go on a date. How long had it been? Six months? Maybe longer than that, I thought. I turned off the water and stepped out of the shower.

Getting dressed for work, I glanced over at the clock. If I didn't step it up, I really was going to be late. I pulled on my boots and ran into the kitchen until I realized there was no time for coffee. I'd just have to get one at work, even though the break room coffee is one step up from drinking actual dirt. This will teach me to over-sleep in the future, I guess... and to not dwell on sexy dreams filled with dark strangers.

Flying out of the door, I ran back inside to grab my umbrella, then flew down the stairs. Once I got outside, I ran up the block, hoping that I hadn't missed my bus. With about twenty seconds to spare, the large red bus rounded the corner and stopped right in front of me. I sighed with relief as I stepped on and sat down in an empty seat. It was only then I realized I hadn't opened my umbrella when I'd gotten outside, and now I was covered in a fine layer of misty rain, causing my skirt and jacket to dampen and making me colder than I actually should be for the duration of the ride. What a great start to the day.

Here we go... I thought to myself as my booted heels clanked slowly but aggressively toward my boss's assistant's office. The feeling of apprehension surrounded me with every step I took on the journey to see the mighty Witch of Oz in her palace. Only this time I was on a different path—a do or die resolve where I wouldn't give in to her demands again.

I was going to start with how distasteful Amanda looked when she tried to glance down her nose at any employee who she thought was beneath her. Didn't she realize she only got as far as she did by sleeping with the head of Dean and Clay Corporation? The only thing I was sure of when I got to her door was that if Amanda decided to lay any more shit at my feet at this hour, just like she had done many times before, hell was going to rain down with the Devil himself as the referee. I was tired of taking on her workload and mine too. Who did she think I was anyway?

"Come in," Amanda called out after I tapped on her door.

I straightened my spine and marched into her spacious office. I would love to work in an office like this; however, I wasn't willing to sell myself like a prostitute to climb the corporate ladder. I'd rather earn it by the sweat of my brow.

"I need to leave in a few minutes, and I have these

files to get out before tomorrow's morning conference meeting, Anna," Amanda immediately informed me before I could open my mouth to say a word.

"Oh," I replied, wondering but suspecting all the same what this had to do with me.

"You can work on the files and place them on Mr. Dean's desk when you're done," she supplied, getting to her feet. She grabbed the pile of manila folders and pushed them at my chest.

I automatically grabbed them before they hit the floor.

"It shouldn't take you no more than three or four hours to get it done," she added.

I really wanted to poke that witch's eye out, but I knew better if I desired to keep my job. "I really can't stay late tonight. I need to—"

A scornful look appeared on Amanda's ivory face, and she cut me off. "Well, if you value your job, Anna—" she rambled, "—you wouldn't turn down this opportunity to prove yourself to the company. You need to try to foster a better employer-employee relationship in this company."

I was put off by Amanda's words. She displayed professional pettiness like a pro.

"I think me working late every night this week so far shows my loyalty to this company, ma'am," I responded, making sure my last word gave an entirely different impression. I forced a grin onto my face. I also had prowess in being petty, although I didn't go there much. I was still spot on and looking overtly polite as I engaged in this mental battle with the slut of Dean & Clay Corporation. In my defense, I wanted to be clear about not wanting to be her patsy any longer.

"In case you have forgotten, I need not remind you I am Mr. Dean's assistant and I have every right to allocate the assignments as I see fit in this company."

I retracted my broad grin to a frown.

There was no way that she really expected me to do all that work. And there was no way that she could really do this to people. I looked up at her. Her look of determinedness thinly veiled the smug expression that really resided on her face. She lived for this kind of thing; taking on a bunch of work and forcing it on her subordinates. She might as well be dumping all of her workload on me, which she basically was doing with the giant stack of papers she had just handed me. A few of them began to fall from my arms and I dipped to catch them. Amanda looked at me, the hint of a smile on her face. She was enjoying every second of my struggle.

Was this really the kind of life I wanted for myself? To be chewed out by people like her? I could've done anything. And yet, here I was standing in an office with an urge to walk over to Amanda's window and throw all of the files out to the wind. But instead, I remained rooted to the spot and completely miserable, thinking about all of the extra time I was going to have to stay here to complete all of this. The office would be completely empty by the time I left. Even the janitors didn't stay that late. At least there were security officers that hung around, although they were most likely just going to be sleeping at their posts. Was this really how I was going to spend my life?

I was young, in my twenties. I should have a life too, but I don't. Cammy is my only friend – and I have no family left to speak of.

My parents had died long ago, and I couldn't remember a time when I wasn't on my own. I had no siblings to speak of, and for the most part I had been alone. I think I'd been at a home for orphaned kids when I was younger, but I couldn't remember any of it. That's what happens sometimes when you experience childhood trauma, or at least that's what a therapist told me once. I had been in and out of the system since I was eighteen, and if you asked me to recall one memory, one single thing that happened in those first eighteen years of my life, I'd be drawing a blank. It was strange, but I lived with it. At least I didn't have a bunch of embarrassing memories from when I was a kid that I would replay over and over in my head like most people did.

I do remember one thing from that time, and that was the longing. The feeling that someone would come and rescue me from whatever situation I was in one day, like a knight on a horse coming in to pick me up and ride off into the sunset together. Like my dream though, it was probably from some fairy tale book I read when I was a kid or a Disney movie. As far as I knew, nothing like that had ever happened to me. No one had ever come for me, no one had ever suddenly remembered that I belonged to them. But for some reason, I held on to a longing that there was someone out there that knew me, and knew that I was theirs.

It was a really dumb idea I held on to for a long time. But once I got a place of my own and started dating, I realized I didn't belong to anyone but myself. The guys I'd been in relationships with were always great at first, but would turn sour pretty quickly. They'd take me to dinner, the movies, a ball game here and there, but it never seemed like it was enough. There was an excitement factor that was missing, and once I realized this, it was pretty much over from there. They never lasted more than a few months, ending in some big argument... and then I'd go running to Cammy, crying about how I could never find the right guy. None of them had ever seemed right. I was still waiting for my knight to come riding up on his horse, and take me away from my mundane, monotonous routine. So far, he was pretty late.

After the last failed attempt, I'd taken a break from dating. But that little break that was supposed to last a few weeks had turned into a few months, and now here I was, single and feeling as if I was always going to be that way. I had forgotten how to talk to men, forgotten how to flirt. I wasn't surprised I hadn't had a date in so long. I don't think I'd want to date me either at the moment.

I had a sorrowful existence of life. Eat, sleep, work, and once a week I would meet with my best friend Cammy. Cammy and I had started at our jobs within a few weeks of each other. Although we both worked in different departments and on different floors of the building, we had been put together a lot as the new hires, having to go through company training and onboarding processes together. After all the mind-numbing paperwork and painful training videos we had to get through, we'd made a bond. She was hilarious, and there was more than one time when we sat at the back of the conference room during company-wide meetings and had to control ourselves from giggling so much, inspiring everyone around us to throw dirty looks our way.

Everyone in the office is either older or married, so we started to gravitate more and more towards one another as two single young women living on their own. I ate my lunch with her down in the cafeteria almost every day like clockwork. I'd have my uncreative salad, and she'd have some interesting leftovers from whatever restaurant she'd been to the night before on a date. I'd started to live vicariously through her, especially since I'd stopped dating. She would tell me all about the different places she'd go, and things they'd do. It was a good way to break up the repetition of most days, hearing about her evenings.

We'd started hanging out after work, getting a drink or two during happy hour. I'd tell her everything I could remember about my life, and she would tell me every-thing about hers. She was much more exciting than I was with all the men she was dating and her confident, take-no-bullshit kind of attitude. She was someone I aspired to be, even if I knew I'd never get there.

She is around my age, and we usually chill at a bar on either a Friday or Saturday night. *What a pathetic life!* She'd tried to set me up with guys she knew, but it never really worked. Either they wouldn't be interested, or I wouldn't. Most of the time it was my interest that wasn't piqued. They just didn't thrill me. But Cammy persevered and kept trying, which I was grateful for, even though I didn't tell her that. It felt nice to have someone care about my life so much.

I looked back to Amanda, remembering that I couldn't blow up at her since she was technically my superior. But what she was asking of me was downright wrong, I knew that she knew it was. I tried to keep my temper in check as I replied.

Amanda cleared her throat bringing me back to the discussion. Her facial expression held a look of impatience.

"Oh, but I think you heard me when I said I can't work late tonight. I never take any time off work, not even when I'm ill." I took a moment to inhale and exhale to calm myself. Amanda really had a way of getting under my skin "According to my calendar, I have plenty of vacation and sick days due. I think I will start taking some days off," I added out of spite.

"Yes, that is correct. But what will you do if you lost your job?" Amanda shot back at me in a threatening tone of voice.

I didn't reply. I clenched my hands into fists. I wondered if steam was coming from my nostrils – that's how furious I felt. The winner of this argument was Amanda yet again. I really disliked her. I bit my bottom lip to keep myself from saying something I might later regret. I wanted to be the winner for once, but I wasn't strong enough to remain firm in my decision.

"The decision is made. You will work overtime tonight," Amanda murmured, swiping her blonde, blunt-cut bangs from her face.

"Pardon," I responded, acting as if I hadn't heard her the first time.

"I said you have to work late and work on the Garnet and Copeland merger files. Make sure they are complete and on Mr. Dean's desk before you leave," she ordered.

"It's storming out, and I'll miss my last bus," I said, hoping Amanda took pity and changed her mind.

"What does a little rain have to do with you completing your work, Anna?" Amanda sneered.

I wanted to ask her if she meant 'her work,' but I didn't. I'm sure karma will have its way with a lowdown, good-for-nothing, mean bitch like her one day soon. But, that wouldn't help at all. Not tonight at least.

She grabbed another stack of files off her desk and dumped them in my already overfilled arms. It was highly calculative of Amanda as she strolled over on ridiculously high heels and intentionally dumped her workload in my arms.

Mr. Dean moseyed into Amanda's office as if on cue. "Are you ready to go, Amanda?" he asked.

If he hadn't walked into her office when he had, I was going to tell her to ram the files up her flat ass. At least I'd thought about it.

"Oh, I didn't see you standing there, Anna," addressed the boss of Dean & Clay Corporation, Mr. Dean.

"Hello, Mr. Dean. I was just—"

"I already set things in play with Anna, and she has agreed to cover for me for the rest of the evening by staying overtime. You must make sure you throw a bonus her way at the end of the month," Amanda said, quickly cutting me off.

I really wanted to call her out on her lies, but I didn't want to risk losing my job. I remained quiet while seething with anger on the inside.

"Anna, thank you," Mr. Dean replied.

I exhaled and looked down at the cream-colored carpeting on the floor, allowing myself to be duped by the lowdown bitch that had slept her way to the top.

"Yeah, thanks, Anna," Amanda chimed in — she spelled it out, dragging every single syllable of my name just the way I hated it.

As I stepped out into the hall, Amanda called out to me. "Hey, Anna! Wait one second."

She grabbed her designer purse and coat, then walked over to me. "Make sure you proofread all of those before you print them. We don't want any typos like last time, remember?"

I plastered a smile on my face, feeling a slight twitch at my temple. "Of course, Amanda."

"Great. You're a pal." She flashed me a dazzling smile and looked over at the boss. "Would you like to see me down to my car, Mr. Dean?"

"With pleasure."

I watched as they walked out of Amanda's office, Mr. Dean's hand at the small of her back, then traveled down even lower. I scrunched up my face in disgust, thankful that I didn't feel the need to dip so low to have an affair with a married man like that. And Mr. Dean had to be well into his fifties. Amanda was my age...did she actually enjoy sleeping with someone almost twice her age?

A few of the files fell from my hands as I struggled to walk back to my desk. Leaning down to pick them up, I couldn't stop thinking about Amanda and her "ambitions" about her job. It wasn't as if she had the best job in the company. Maybe she did make more than most assistants, but it wasn't as if she was the head of the company by now, or anywhere near it. Did she think Mr. Dean was going to get divorced and marry her so she could be a trophy wife for the rest of her life?

I thought about his wife and three grown kids at home. He was never going to leave her...they'd been married for like thirty years or something. Did his wife know? Amanda and the boss had been sleeping together for several months as far as I knew. Everyone in the office knew about their arrangement, and it had become just another normal piece of gossip amongst our coworkers.

They barely hid it when they were at the office together, especially that last moment where Mr. Dean had grabbed her ass. It's almost as if they didn't care anymore. His wife had to know... they got a hotel room at least three or four nights a week, and she accompanied him on every business trip he went on. I'm just happy that it's her, and not me. I don't know how I could live with myself, living a life like that.

I walked back over to my desk and sat down, spilling the files all over the place. It would take me an extra fifteen minutes just to get everything organized. Glancing up at the large clock on the wall, I sighed. It would be nice to have a bonus at the end of the month, if Mr. Dean even remembered. I sincerely doubted that Amanda would remind him.

Logging back onto my computer and letting it boot

up, I watched as the office emptied out, everyone going home to relax and unwind for the evening. That could've been me, I thought. If I'd just fought it enough, maybe Amanda would've found someone else to do the work. No way, I thought. She had it out for me, and she loved giving me extra work, because she knew it made my life miserable. One of these days, she was going to get what was coming to her, I thought to myself.

But until that day, I'd be stuck picking up her heavy workload. The sad thing was, even if I was on my way home like everyone else, I didn't have anything to do. I didn't have a pet so I didn't have to get home and feed them. I didn't have a boyfriend so I didn't have a dinner or a date to rush off to. All I'd do when I got home was watch TV until I fell asleep, like I did every night. Well, except for the weekends when I'd go out with Cammy. Tomorrow night, to be exact, when we'd go out and get some drinks, forgetting all about this horrible week. And it couldn't come soon enough, I thought to myself as I started sifting through the mess of files on my desk.

CHAPTER TWO
ANNA

"AND, DONE!"

I hit the print button on the screen in front of me and rubbed the back of my neck. After sitting for so long, I was really feeling the ache in my neck and back. What I wouldn't give to go home right now to some big strapping man that could pour me a glass of wine and give me a massage. I chuckled to myself. I've been reading way too many romance novels lately.

I stood up and stretched my arms over my head, then walked down the hall to retrieve the report from the printer. The office was slightly eerie at night, with its rows of empty cubicles and soft whirring of everyone's computers. It would be the perfect setting for a horror movie.

Why did I have to think like that? I asked myself. I was going to get all worked up and freak myself out over nothing. Everything was fine, I just happened to be alone in a huge building at night. There was nothing scary about it. There weren't any goblins or monsters waiting to jump out at me as I rounded the corner. I was a grown adult, and I knew better. At least that's what I told myself.

The streets are nearly deserted by the time I leave work. I take off at a fast-paced walk as the first drops of rain land on my back. The weatherman didn't even predict rain for tonight, but you could smell it in the air. I had already missed the bus that would take me to my apartment. Mr. Dean had kept me past eight o'clock doing work that his assistant should have been doing. Everyone at Dean and Clay Corporation knew that Mr. Dean was fucking Amanda.

The icy, dark sky rumbled, and the rain grew heavier. The sidewalk was slick, and the rain continued beating against my body, making me wet. At least my feet would remain dry thanks to my knee-high leather boots. I shivered. The cold was getting worse. It was late October, and I foolishly got caught in the downpour because I didn't have the extra money to pay the exorbitant cab fare. My living expenses had taken much of my paycheck.

Goosebumps rose on my flesh. The coat I had on wasn't any help against the chilly wetness from the rain. I inhaled and exhaled. My breath became clouded in the air. At least I had only five more blocks to go before I arrived at my apartment building.

I should've gone around the longer way. This street, although busy during the day, was completely deserted at night. All of the businesses had long since closed for the evening, and not a single car drove down the street as I kept up my pace. I really should start carrying something to protect myself...a single female alone in the city. At least a can of mace in my purse would be a good thing to have if I found myself in a sticky situation, kind of like this one. Or a knife? A gun would be too much, I think. I'd be scared to even carry one around, let alone actually use it if someone tried to mess with me.

If I'd just walked down the next street over, I could've walked by restaurants and bars full of people. That would've made me feel much better than walking down this dark and empty street. I was usually good about keeping myself out of situations like this, but I was exhausted and just wanted to get home.

Hopefully, I hadn't made a huge mistake by not getting a cab. Hopefully I could just get home without any problem. I hurried down the sidewalk, my boots splashing in puddles as the unrelenting rain continued to gather on the ground. One lone street light flickered at the end of the road, and I kept my eyes fixed on it. I told myself that if I reached the light, I'd be ok. The next street down was a bit more busy than this one, and I'd be ok. I just had to reach that street light first.

Suddenly, footfalls thumped behind me. I whirled around so fast I almost lost my footing. My heart rate increased, and my first instinct was to scream when I faced the unflinching, unblinking stranger who stood menacingly before me. His face was hard looking under the night light. I gulped when my gaze trailed down to see the knife the thief grasped. The knife was being toyed within his hand and it glimmered in the downpour.

The man spoke with a nasal tone of voice. "Give me your purse—now."

"No!" I screamed, frantically looking around for someone to help me. I was the only one foolish enough to be caught out in this storm on a dark and dreary night such as this. *Damn... damn... damn!* Instead, I stood there visibly shaking in a state of paralyzing unease.

"Lady, I'm not playing fucking games. Give me your purse now."

A profound sense of determination burst forth within me. *Run*, my mind screamed. Finally, I gathered my strength and turned to run. By the sound behind me,

I knew he took off in pursuit. I was not a runner but I silently prayed for the speed of Flo Jo. My breath spurted from my mouth in terror.

"Please, God, let me live…" I cried silently, throwing myself ahead with even larger abandon.

Bam! It was like I'd run into a brick wall. I would have fallen flat on my face if random arms that felt like steel hadn't reached out to grab me. They stopped me from falling onto the wet, cold, hard pavement. I couldn't see anything but the wide expanse of a chest in front of me, and I knew whoever held me was tall; much taller and bigger than the thief pursuing me. An exotic, seductive smell invaded my nostrils.

I was so frightened that I felt sick. I uncontrollably shivered, and my head felt light and airy. My vision started to become unclear. The eerie darkness was lit by dim streetlights. A hissing noise followed by a low growl above me had me opening my mouth in a silent scream. My awareness was fluctuating at a fast pace. I tried to breathe through the nauseated feeling overtaking me, but I wasn't having much luck.

"Oh my God! What kind of fucking monster are you?" The man behind me yelled.

"Leave this woman alone or I will kill you," the ominous voice above me rumbled. No more words came from the would-be mugger.

Receding footsteps ran in the opposite direction. Throughout the interchange of words, my heartbeat pounded deafeningly, reverberating in my ears.

"Who are you?" I tried to glance up into the stranger's face, but my eyes closed, and I faded into darkness.

I opened my weary eyes and let out a yawn. I was so tired. I turned my head toward the streak of brightness filtering through the room. Sunlight shone through the slit in the printed flowered curtains. I sat up in bed and rubbed my eyes. *Wait, how did I get in my bedroom in my apartment?* Was last night all a dream? No, it couldn't be... I looked under the bed covers and gasped aloud. I was completely nude. I had never slept in the nude in my life.

Memories of last night were vague but they slowly attempted to emerge in my head. I remembered being confronted by a man demanding my handbag. I remembered running—and then not much else. *Why couldn't I remember?* I glanced over at my bedside clock and noted the time.

Blasted! It was seven-thirty, and I need to get dressed for work. I was glad today was Friday. That meant my best friend Cammy and I could get together for a drink and relax later on tonight. I hopped out of the bed and hurriedly prepared for my day at Dean and

Clay Corporation. I was one of the ones who got saddled with the work that no one else wanted to do. I couldn't complain much because my job did pay the bills and it was the only one I had for now. Maybe I should go back to college and work on getting my bachelor's Degree. *I could move higher in the company plus make more money*, I thought on my way to the bus stop.

And that way I'd be out of Amanda's reach, and she couldn't tell me to do her extra work for her. If I moved up, then maybe I'd be telling her what to do, and make her stay late so she missed her bus. I doubt she even took the bus, but it didn't matter in the scenario I had in my head, which included me berating her for doing less than exemplary work. She would apologize profusely, and tell me she'll make sure it won't happen again. I smiled at the thought, and rounded the corner to the bus stop.

There's a big crowd waiting when I get there. Great, it's running late. I look up at the digital screen with bus times above the bench. The bus will be here in two minutes, but will I even get a seat? I think about taking a cab to work, but talk myself out of it. It was just too expensive, and I wasn't going to be late to work. I would be there right on time, if this bus really came when it was supposed to.

Three minutes later, the bus came rolling down

the street. It was almost empty inside and I breathed a sigh of relief. The crowd had grown even bigger as everyone waited impatiently in line to board. I was towards the front of the line thankfully. When I finally got on, I was lucky enough to snag one of the last seats. I sat down next to an older woman who gave me a polite smile then looked out the window.

I followed her gaze. It was a dreary, gray morning and definitely looked like it was going to rain later. I should've brought my umbrella.

Sitting back in my seat, I notice that the bus driver has the heat cranked up and I'm thankful for it. It wasn't exactly freezing outside, but the heat certainly helped to take the chill away. I leaned back and rested my eyes for a moment.

I was walking down the dark, deserted street when the mugger stepped in front of me, demanding that I give him my purse. I refused and tried to get away. He stepped forward, holding up a knife and told me again to hand over my purse. I took off running, running, the mugger close on my heels when I ran straight into a solid wall of flesh. Dazed, I glanced up and looked straight into the eyes of–

"Hello, dear."

I woke abruptly to the old lady next to me shaking

my arm. I had fallen asleep and leaned right onto her shoulder.

"Oh, I'm so sorry!" I looked at her apologetically.

"That's alright. We all could use an extra nod off here and there." She smiled warmly. I smiled back and looked out the window. I was almost at my stop. I stood up and walked to the front of the bus, waiting to get off. The dream I'd been having was so vivid, and yet seemed so familiar. My mind was a cloudy mess as I stepped off the bus and down the block to my office.

Later on, I sat in my cubicle and wished the day would end as I did my sorting of files. I need coffee, but it isn't yet time for my break. I always struggle through my day until lunchtime.

After I finished sorting the files and caught up on a few emails, I glanced up at the large clock on the wall. It was time for my break, and I was more than ready to get up and walk around. I stood up and stretched, trying to stifle a yawn as I walked down the hall to the breakroom. I still felt exhausted, and knew that a cup of coffee was what I needed.

It must be because I worked so late, I think to myself as I pour the ground coffee into the filter and hit the button to start brewing. I couldn't remember what time I got home, but it must've been much later than I realized. That's why I was so tired, I tell myself. I sat down at a table and looked out the window, waiting for the coffee to finish.

It was another cold, gray day outside, and I wondered if we'd ever see another sunny day again. It rained a lot this time of year, but I really could've used a reprieve from the precipitation for at least one day. I guess it didn't matter, since I spent most of my time inside...from the office, to my apartment, and back again. Except for tonight. I looked forward to seeing Cammy at lunch, so we could finalize our plans for going out later. It was the only thing I had to look forward to all day.

The coffee maker started beeping to let me know it was finished, and I got up to pour myself a cup. As I swallowed the bitter-tasting coffee down as quickly as I could, I heard a pair of heels clicking on the tiled floor behind me. Turning around in my chair to see who had joined me in the breakroom, my face fell. It was Amanda. She walked over to the fridge and grabbed a bottle of water.

"Coffee? You know it's not good to put so many stimulants in your body, right? I try to drink only water and stay away from caffeine."

"Well, that's great for you, Amanda. If only the rest of us could be so lucky."

She smiled smugly and walked over to the door. "Oh, by the way, good job on those files last night."

I looked up at her, surprised by the compliment. "Thank you."

"Of course, there were a few things that you did mess up."

"There were?" I ask her in an even tone while taking another sip of coffee, and resisting the urge to throw it at her.

"Yes, but don't worry. I made sure everything was fixed before I sent them off to the higher-ups. They were so pleased with the work I did on them."

"The work *you* did on them?" I crossed my arms and raised my eyebrows in surprise that she would say that to me. I had spent literally hours finishing up all that work, and now she was getting the credit. I guess I should've expected it, especially coming from her.

"Well, yeah, Anna. I couldn't tell them you did it... how would that make me look? But, that's why I'm really thankful to you and everything you did for me. I'll make sure that Mr. Dean knows that too."

"I'm sure you will."

"What was that?"

"Nothing, Amanda. Thanks, I guess."

"You're very welcome. I have to fly out for a business trip with Mr. Dean next week, and we'll probably be gone up until Friday. But, there's a few deadlines coming up, and so I'll have some more work for you to do. You won't mind a few late nights again, will you? Remember, I'll tell Mr. Dean about all of your hard work!" Amanda flashed me a sickly-sweet smile. All I could do was stare at her.

"We'll talk about it on Monday. I don't want to take up any more of your break, which is almost over, right? Got to get back to work!" She smiled again as she walked out of the breakroom. I sighed and took another sip of my coffee, which had gone cold in the time Amanda had talked to me. It was just as well, I thought. I hated drinking it anyways. I got up and went back to my desk, trying to throw myself back into work.

Finally, lunchtime has arrived. I strolled into the cafeteria that's located in the basement of the building. My friend Cammy waves at me and I wave back before heading over to get myself a chicken sandwich and a coffee. I paid for my items at the cash register and headed over to sit at the table with my friend. At least the coffee in the cafeteria was better than it was upstairs.

Cammy is gorgeous and curvaceous. She can get any man she sets her mind to. I think it's her outgoing personality. I wasn't as much to look at like Cammy was. I stood five feet and two inches tall with big brown eyes. I wasn't near as curvy as my friend. But I did have flawless dark brown skin. Not a pimple in sight!

"Hey girl, are you ready for tonight?" Cammy asked.

"Yes," I sighed.

"What's wrong, honey? You look tired."

"I am. I was pulled from the pool of secretaries to work late last night just when my shift was over."

"Let me guess. Mr. Dean's assistant Amanda had you doing her job again, I suppose." Cammy knew how Amanda was. I honestly think the woman had it in for me, but I had no idea why.

"You already know it. I bet Mr. Dean took her to some fancy swanky restaurant while I was slaving away in the office."

"Hmm, I wonder what Mrs. Dean would do if she found out her husband was fucking his assistant?" Cammy asked in a low tone of voice.

"She probably would take him for everything he was worth. Isn't her father a judge?"

"I heard he was. I also heard that's how Mr. Dean was able to open up Dean and Clay with the backing of Judge Parkland. At least that's the rumor," Cammy went on to say.

"Wow," I looked on in interest as Cammy spoke. I shoved the last bit of my sandwich into my mouth before I spoke. "I don't know, don't you think Mrs. Dean already suspects something? I mean, she accompanies him on all of his business trips, he takes her out to these expensive restaurants all the time, and he basically has a standing reservation for a hotel room downtown."

"Maybe she just turns a blind eye to it. But, if I was the daughter of a judge and my husband was cheating on me, I'd take him for everything he's got."

"I know you would, Cammy." I tried to stifle a yawn but was unsuccessful.

"Geez, they really are working you too hard up there. And keeping you way too late."

"I had to walk home in that thunderstorm last night. I almost got mugged," I divulged.

Cammy's mouth opened and closed but no words came out. Her brown colored skin grew darker, her eyes widened and both brows were frozen in a high arch. I picked up my coffee cup and took a long fortifying drink. Cammy continued to sit across the table from me in stunned silence.

"You got to be fucking kidding me," Cammy finally said.

"No, I'm not kidding you. I was so scared."

"How did that happen? And why the hell were you walking alone at that time of the night? Especially in the rain?" Cammy questioned me with a look of concern on her pretty face.

"I missed the bus. I would have had to wait at least

an hour for the next one to come along. I was only five blocks from my apartment when it happened."

"You should have called a damn cab, Anna."

"I know. I guess I wasn't thinking. I will never do such a stupid thing again," I replied.

"You're damn right that was stupid! I could have lost you. I could have woken up this morning with the news of you murdered in some alleyway. I'm so mad at you right now," Cammy's brown eyes fumed with anger.

"I'm disappointed in myself to allow myself to get in that situation, so I understand your anger. The good news is that the wannabe mugger didn't get my purse. Can you imagine if he got ahold of my identification... He would have known where I lived, had my credit card information, everything."

"Sheesh! How did you avoid him taking your purse and did you call the police?" Cammy asked.

"No, I didn't call the police. To be honest, I don't quite remember every detail about last night. I remember running as fast as I could and then I bumped into someone. Girl, it was like hitting a wall. I don't remember how the man chasing me looked. Everything happened so fast. But, I do remember the man's smell I ran into, and the sound of his voice. I didn't see a face. He smelled like lavender; something exotic and very dark. I don't remember anything else. I woke up at my apartment, naked in bed and alone. Cammy, I don't remember how I got there. It's disconcerting, and I don't know if I'm going crazy or if I just dreamt it all."

Cammy looked at me and shook her head. "I don't like the sound of that at all. Are you sure you don't remember anything else? This wasn't just some crazy dream you had, was it?"

I thought about it for a moment. "The funny thing is, it felt like a dream but I know it was real. Even though there's no proof. Nothing of mine is missing, and my apartment looked alright when I woke up. It was locked from the inside like I always do, so there's really no possible way anyone was in there."

"Do you think maybe you had something in your system that made you...altered?" Cammy asked me. "What if you got slipped something, like a pill that made you black out?"

"Are you talking about the date rape drug? Wouldn't I have woken up somewhere else if someone had slipped me something? If I passed out, I couldn't see me getting myself home and climbing into bed. There's got to be some other explanation."

Cammy looked like she was thinking hard about it. "And you're sure you didn't stop somewhere on the way home and have a drink?"

"No, I went straight home from work; I didn't have a

drop of alcohol yesterday, although it feels like I did." I tried to hide a yawn as I spoke.

"Well, you've got me stumped. I can't think of anything else other than being drunk or drugged up that could make you act like that."

"Yeah, it's kind of freaking me out."

"I need a strong drink," Cammy sighed, and gave me a pitying look.

"You and me both," I sat back heavily in my seat and prayed that I wasn't going mad.

I yawned again, this time without hiding it. I was pretty tired, like I'd been up all night. Wouldn't I have remembered more if I'd been conscious, though? I'd had nights before where I was a little fuzzy on the memories, but I'd never forgotten hours and hours of time before. Maybe when I was running away from the mugger, I hit my head and fell. Maybe I had a concussion. I reached up and patted my head, feeling around for any bruises or bumps. Nothing felt lumpy or sensitive to the touch.

I sat back, even more confused now than when I had sat down in the first place. Maybe I really was going mad.

"Well, I guess I should get back to my desk if I'm going to finish all of my work, because one thing I will not be doing is staying late again."

"That's right, girl. We've got plans later. Does 8:00

still work for you?" Cammy stood up and looked at me hopefully.

"Eight o'clock works for me. You couldn't stop me from going out tonight... I'll need a big, strong one when I get there."

"A drink, or a man?" Cammy looked at me slyly.

I laughed. "A drink to start, then we'll see where the night takes us."

Before I get back to my desk, I head into the bathroom. It was empty, and I was thankful for that. I walked over to the sink and absentmindedly washed my hands as I replayed last night's events over again in my head. Everything was the same, and nothing new was popping up. If I could just figure out how I got home and got into bed, then I wouldn't be so freaked out. It's so unlike me to forget that much...maybe I was coming down with something.

I looked up in the mirror and moved my head around, checking for any unseen marks or bruises I hadn't seen before. But there was nothing there. I looked exactly like I did the day before, and the day before that. Just with a little extra worry line forming across my forehead.

The only explanation was the man that had saved me had taken me home. Was I so overcoming with shock that I told a complete stranger my address and how to get me up to my apartment? And then why was I naked? Did I have sex with him? I couldn't even remember the last time I had sex. Maybe my clothes had gotten ruined somehow and I threw them off without grabbing anything else to sleep in. It all seemed so strange. I yawned again and leaned against the sink. All I knew was something wasn't adding up, and it was really bugging me that I couldn't put the pieces back together.

I bent down and splashed some water on my face. The cool droplets on my skin helped to calm my nerves for a few moments. What I needed was a nap, I thought. And maybe a long hot soak in a tub with a bottle of wine. Maybe I should cancel with Cammy and do that instead tonight. It would probably do me some good to stay at home and get a restful night's sleep.

"No, you're going out tonight," I said to myself in the mirror. I had to put some normalcy back in my routine, and weekends were for going out with Cammy and getting drinks. Nothing was going to stop me from going forward with my plans, even if I was going to think most of the night about this mystery man, and how I had gotten home. Maybe a few drinks would help me jog my memory.

I chuckled at that and grabbed a paper towel to dry my face off. Just a few more hours to go, and I'd be out of here. I threw the papers in the trash and walked out of the bathroom, taking a breath and putting myself back to rights. Amanda was coming down the hall from the boss' office from the opposite end, and I had to fight the urge to trip her. She smiled smugly at me as she passed by me. Without smiling back, I ducked into my cubicle and sat down at my desk, ready to get all of my work finished for the week.

CHAPTER THREE
ANNA

I LOOKED up from my computer screen, feeling the strain on my eyes when I noticed it was just about time to end things for the day. I leaned back and stretched, happy to say goodbye to this week. And now I could go out and have drinks with Cammy and unwind.

I tidied up my desk and turned my computer off then grabbed my purse and my coat. Everyone else was packing up for the day as I passed by cubicle after cubicle.

"Have a good night, Anna!" A coworker called out as I walked down the hallway.

"You too, Anthony!" I almost made my way to the elevators when there was one more door I had to pass by; Amanda's. I walked briskly, watching out of the corner of my eye as I went.

Amanda and Mr. Clay were in there, him casually leaning on her desk and her looking up at him and batting her eyes while wearing a very low-cut shirt. Really, I was glad I wasn't in her place. I definitely didn't want to be sleeping with a married man twice my age all to get ahead in life. No, I was fine with my position, for once.

Luckily they don't see me walk by and I make it to the elevator without being stopped by anyone. I just knew that Amanda would've had no problem with assigning me to come in on Saturday and do some extra work. I walked into the elevator and breathed a sigh of relief. The next two days belonged to me. It was time to switch off work mode, and go home and get ready to go out. I had a cute new miniskirt I was dying to wear out, and I was determined to have a good night, even if it just involved me and Cammy getting tipsy over cocktails. It was much better than anything else that had happened this week.

Leaving at my normal end time, I walked to the bus stop and waited a few minutes with all of the other commuters. The bus pulled up right on time and I walked in, finding a seat and looking out the window. Someone sat down next to me, but I didn't even look to see who the person was. I was ready to go and unwind at home for a few hours before meeting up with Cammy.

I counted the stops the bus made until it was finally my turn. Getting up, I got off and walked the short distance to my apartment building. The sidewalk was pretty crowded, but I wasn't surprised. It was the end of the week, and people were hurrying to get home. I was happy for the crowd, really. It was much better to be bumping into people than to be walking alone on an empty, deserted street. I got to my building and climbed the steps to my apartment, locking the door behind me.

The first thing I did was kick off my shoes and pull off my pantyhose underneath my skirt. Since I lived alone, it didn't matter too much how I walked around. I could be completely naked laying on the couch if I wanted, even though I never did that. That's why last night was so strange. I had never slept naked in my entire life.

I changed into sweatpants and warmed up a frozen dinner in the microwave. It would be good to have something on my stomach when I had drinks later, and it was cheaper to eat at home. I turned on the TV and ate, watching some mindless reality show until it was time to start getting ready for the evening.

Pouring myself a glass of wine, I jumped into the shower, washing away the day. I was determined to have a fun, carefree night with Cammy, and I wasn't going to let my nagging questions about last night ruin my time. I reached out and flipped on the radio on the shelf, drowning out my thoughts and singing along loudly to some 90's R&B song.

After I was done, I wrapped a towel around me and walked over to the closet where my brand new miniskirt was hanging up, waiting for me. I grabbed it along with a pair of black hose and a halter top. I was going to go all out tonight, I told myself. I spent a little longer than usual on my makeup, making my eyes more dramatic than usual. I topped off the look with some gold hoop earrings. Zipping up my knee-length boots, I stood up and walked over to the mirror, turning this way and that.

I looked good. Better than good. I looked hot, and I couldn't wait to get out and have some fun. Club Mist always had a good mix of people, and they played great music. I was going to have some drinks and dance my butt off and flirt with some cute guys. It was going to be a great night, and completely normal, I told myself. Looking over at the clock, I realized it was time to go. I grabbed my purse and headed for the door, finishing the last few drops of my wine as I went.

It was eight p.m. on a Friday evening when I emerged from the taxi and walked into the bar. I peered through the dim interior of the building looking for Cammy. She had texted me no more than fifteen minutes ago telling me to meet her at the club. She wanted to pick me up, but I told her no. I couldn't live in fear of navigating the city where I grew up. I pushed fear aside and hailed a taxi to Club Mist.

A cold shiver ran down my spine, and the fine hairs on the back of my neck stood on end.

"Anna," a deep voice echoed through my head. Despite the music blasting from the surround sound speakers, I could hear my name being called. A rich, deep and potent aroma wafted through my nostrils. The smell was familiar to me. I spun around on my heel to locate the person calling my name. A hand settled on my shoulder and I let loose a squeaking sound that was deafened by the music.

"Hey, Anna. It's just me." My friend Cammy walked around to face me. "I didn't mean to frighten you. Last night still has you spooked, huh? You need to calm down."

"Oh my God! I almost peed my panties," I gasped, my hand flew to my chest. Cammy took my other hand in hers and led me over to the bar.

"You need a drink, honey," she said. Cammy pushed me toward an empty barstool then took a seat beside me.

"Shit. I need two or three of them. Just before you came up to me, I swear I heard a man calling my name."

"You're hearing things, Anna. You couldn't even hear me calling your name before I tried to get your attention. What do you want to drink? Tonight, drinks are on me," Cammy's eyes held a look of concern.

"Thanks, girl. Get me a rum and coke. I need something strong."

I wasn't having any of those fruity drinks that I usually went for. Cammy wasted no time in gaining the bartender's attention and ordered our drinks.

I looked over my shoulder; I felt like I was being watched but I didn't see anyone out of the ordinary. "Here you go," Cammy said, and I swiveled around in my seat to take a sip from my drink. It was strong, and I embraced the warmth sliding down my throat.

"That's just what I needed," I stated. I took another long sip hoping the alcohol would settle my nerves.

I started to rock back and forth in my chair to the beat of the music. Cammy took notice and grabbed my hand.

"Let's dance."

We wandered over to the dance floor and began to dance, moving my body to the rhythm. There weren't too many dancers out here yet, but it was still early. It gave me some elbow room though to sip my drink and take a look around the room. Although I didn't really recognize any of the faces I saw, I couldn't shake the feeling like I was being watched. I turned in a full circle, trying to see if anyone was staring at me from a dark-ened corner or something.

"What is it? Do you see someone we know?"

"No. Hey, can you take this back for me? I've got to hit the bathroom."

I handed my drink to Cammy and walked off the dance floor and over to the women's restroom. A few girls were in there fixing their lipstick and talking about guys as I walked into and locked myself into a stall. Finally, I felt safer. What was going on with me?

Maybe I really was losing it. Ever since getting almost mugged last night, I felt like there was someone out to get me at every turn. At least in here, I didn't have to worry about that. And Cammy was right outside, waiting for me. I was perfectly fine, and there was nothing to worry about. That's what I kept telling myself anyway.

Walking over to the sink, I splash some water onto the back of my neck and my chest, feeling the warmth of the club and being out on the dance floor, as well as sipping on strong drinks start to get to me. I'd have to pace myself if I was going to go all night. I'd order a water when I went back out, along with another drink of course.

"He was definitely looking at me."

"Are you sure he wasn't checking me out? The tall

guy with the long hair? I think he was looking at me way before he noticed you."

I chuckled to myself as two drunk girls fought about some guy over by the hand dryers. I walked out and back over to Cammy. Thankfully, Cammy and I never had that problem. We had different tastes in men, which made it easier for us to go out together. Not that I ever really ended up talking to anyone. It was always Cammy that was getting the guys.

Just like right now. As I got to our seats, Cammy was talking to a guy on the other side of her. I slipped back onto my bar stool and finished the last remnants of my drink, then ordered another and a glass of ice water. I watched out of the corner of my eye as the guy walked away from Cammy, giving her a wink. She turned back to me and smiled.

"Well, this night just got interesting."

"Oh yeah, are you madly in love?" I joked with her as I sipped on my water.

"Maybe. At least for the night."

I laughed. "That's a good way to look at it. I wish I could look at men the same way you do."

"You can, it's all about that confidence, girl. Don't worry, we'll work on it. And you look hot tonight. You could probably get any guy in here."

"I don't know about that."

"I do. You've just gotta flaunt it, like me. Take a look around the room. Do you see anyone that looks interesting?"

I swung around on my stool and looked around the bar. The dance floor was starting to fill out, and more people were beginning to arrive. But as I looked around the room, I seemed to find a problem with every man I saw...too young, too short, too bald...no one really stood out.

"There's no one really here that looks very exciting."

Cammy laughed. "You might be right about that."

"Maybe I should just go home. I don't know if I'm really feeling it tonight."

"Take a few more sips, and then we'll go back out on the dance floor. You love dancing! It always puts you in a better mood."

I smiled at her. "You're right. I need to shake off this dull mood I'm in, and get more into the spirit."

"That's my girl. Cheers!" She held up her glass and clinked it against mine.

I took another long sip and looked around the room again, trying to see if anyone new had walked in since I'd last checked. I suppose there were a few cute guys around, and some of them even glanced my way. I had to admit I did look pretty good tonight, despite my reluctance to let loose and have a good time.

If only I could meet someone exciting and daring. Most of the men here seemed like they'd get boring after a while. And I could say the same about most of the men in this city. Everyone started to blend together...wearing the same style of clothes, drinking the same kind of beer, playing the same game of pool over and over. I wanted someone different. Someone unique. And since I knew that I definitely wasn't going to be finding anyone that fit that description tonight, I chose to focus on having fun instead.

"Should we go back out to the dance floor?"

"Yeah, maybe. I don't want to lose our seats though. I wish there was a way we could save them."

The bar was starting to fill up, and people were coming up on either side of us to order their cocktails from the bartender. All of a sudden, the feeling of being watched came over me again. The hairs on the back of my neck stood up, and I shuddered as if someone had just walked over my grave.

Cammy leaned over in her seat, placed her lips close to my ear, and whispered, "Don't look now but there is a tall muscular, gorgeous man, around thirtyish or so on your left staring at you." I start to turn my head but Cammy elbows me in the side. "Don't look now silly. I'll tell you when to look."

"Okay, but don't elbow me that hard again. I bet I have a bruise on my side in the morning." I giggled.

Cammy laughed and took a sip from her mixed drink. "Oh—Oh, you can look now," she informed me with excitement dripping from her voice. I took another sip from my drink before turning my head in the direction that Cammy had indicated. I saw the back of a tall man with thick dark long hair that swept mid-way down his back. His face was unusually pale, but that didn't stop him from being handsome. I straightened in my seat when his head whipped around and our eyes collided. I could swear his eyes lit up as he stared at me. A tremble sizzled through my body and shook my entire frame. *How did this strikingly handsome stranger cause all these emotions to go through my system?* I grew weak, and I could swear I heard my name called again.

"Anna," Cammy nudged me to garner my attention.

"What?" I reluctantly tore my gaze away from the sexy stranger.

"Do you know that man?"

"No," I replied. "I have never seen him a day in my life." My gaze on its own accord seemed to be drawn back to the man, but he was gone. A sudden feeling of sadness overwhelmed me. The fine hairs on the back of my neck stood on end, again. Cammy gasped beside me and gave me another jab to my side. A wide smile covered her pretty face when I looked over at her. Cammy jerked her head in a direction behind me; then I heard his voice.

"Hello," the voice rumbled. It was like thunder but melted over me like warm butter.

I couldn't resist. I swiveled myself around on the barstool and looked up—up—and up. My mouth opened and closed as a familiar feeling overwhelmed me along with the smell of lavender. A long-labored sigh expelled itself from my lips. My eyes raked up and down across a wide and muscular chest. He was at least six-foot and five inches in height.

"Hey," I stuttered, finally finding my voice. My gaze returned to his gorgeous face. His ice grey eyes held me entranced.

Cammy gave a girlish giggle, but I could not tear my eyes away from the man standing before me. He stood in my presence as if waiting for something. It seemed like I was supposed to remember something important, but whatever it was slipped from my memory.

"Anastasia, I've found you at last. My beloved, you belong to me," the voice echoed through my mind.

Only one fact came to my awareness. I was surely losing my mind. "I need to use the restroom," I said to no one in particular and hopped down from the stool.

"Wait," the word resonated through my brain, and I froze mid-step.

"Anna are you okay?" Cammy was by my side in minutes. Almost immediately, the stranger was consuming my space again and I couldn't breathe. My heart beats erratically against my chest. I looked up into the light reflection of his eyes and I was lost.

"Leave us at once," he said to Cammy, turning his head to address her. My friend opened her mouth as if to speak, but no words came out. She stood with a frozen look on her face and nodded as she headed back toward the bar without another word.

I tried to take off after Cammy. "Cammy, wait!" I yelled, but she kept walking.

The strange man loomed over me. I tried to take a step back, but he wasn't having it.

"Anastasia, I've found you at last." The stranger said, gripping my hand in his much larger one. He started to tug me toward the exit of the building.

"Let me go! Let me go right this minute," I demanded. I tried to dig my heels into the carpeted floor but to no avail. We were by the door now and I caught the eye of a security guard. "Help me," I begged. "I'm being kidnapped." No one paid attention to my distress. It was as if the crowd was wrapped up in their own universe.

"Have a good night, Mr. Masters," said the security guard. He looked as if nothing was happening out of the ordinary. I glanced back toward the bar to see Cammy sitting in the same spot we occupied earlier. She was talking to a man and laughing as if she had forgotten about me. *How could my best friend be sitting there like that without calling for help? Didn't Cammy realize what was happening to me?* It seems I was on my own.

I kicked and yelled until the man swept me up into his arms and hauled me over his shoulders like a sack of potatoes. I balled my hands into fists and beat as hard as I could against his back, but it was like hitting against a brick wall.

"Stop, beloved. You will only hurt yourself," he said. His deep voice had lowered to a seductive growl.

He came to a halt outside on the cold street. People stopped to stare but a loud hiss emanated through the night and the people went scurrying away like frightened mice. He stopped at a long black limousine with dark tinted windows. "I understand, you may be afraid, Anastasia. But do not be. I will not harm you. I would never harm my wife."

"You're lying!" I shouted. "I'm no one's wife. Let me go you lunatic." I barely got the words out when a thin, tall and pale man in a black suit emerged from the driver's side of the car. He walked around and opened the back passenger side door. I was placed inside by this psychotic man. Mr. Masters, as he has been known, soon joined me before the door was closed and we took out into the night.

I blinked a few times until my eyes became used to the low light. The glare from the street lights could hardly be seen through the heavily-tinted windows. The inside of the limo was lined with seats covered in a soft, dark red leather. There was a bar to one side with a marble countertop. I looked up to the sunroof. It was also heavily tinted. If this was any other situation, I would've been impressed by the expensive-looking surroundings. But instead, I saw this limo as a prison from which I had to escape.

Looking around, I tried to find controls for the windows. There were none. This car looked like it had been made for picking up wayward women and seducing them into doing whatever this lunatic wished. Well, that was not going to be me. I needed to find a way out of here, and I needed to find a way out now.

There had to be a way to open the windows at least. Wouldn't you want to feel a breeze once in a while?

He spoke to the driver, saying a phrase quickly in a language I didn't understand. Who was this guy? Was he in the mafia, or something? Or was he something worse... an expert kidnapper that had the power to control minds and make people turn away when the other is crying for help. No, I thought. That's ridiculous.

But what were his plans for me? Was I a victim of human trafficking? I had seen news shows about it... a woman is just walking down the street, and the next things she knows she is being grabbed and thrown into the back of a van, carted off to some other part of the world to be a sex slave. This wasn't the back of a van, but the situation definitely felt dangerous. My life was in danger, and I had to get out of here.

I reached for my purse to grab my phone, but it wasn't there. It was back at the bar, sitting on top of the stool where I had just been having drinks with Cammy. I could still taste the rum and coke I had been sipping. How was it possible that my life had been so normal mere minutes ago? In the blink of an eye everything had completely changed.

I wish that I had never come out tonight. It was too soon after that brutal attack the night before. My guard must've been down or something. I should've just called Cammy and told her to come over for a movie night. We could've sat at my apartment ordering a pizza and drinking wine and had a safe, normal night. But no, I had to prove it to myself that I was capable of going out without being harmed. Well, that obviously wasn't the case now. I didn't even know what the guy was going to do to me yet; that might be the scariest part of all. He just kept saying I was someone I wasn't. How do I get out of this hellish nightmare?

I inched away from him on the seat to the other side of the car. It didn't do much, because he just moved with me. The way he looked at me...his eyes were full of passion and longing. I felt a slight tug of heat in my belly, which surprised me. Here I was, in the grip of certain death, and my body was having a strange reaction of lust to this madman.

I wiped any thoughts of desire from my head, and replaced them with anger. "Sir, I don't know who you think I am, but I'm not her. My name is Anna. I'm a secretary, a really low-level one. I live in a crappy one-bedroom apartment, and go out with my best friend Cammy on the weekends. That's all I do. I have never seen you before in my life, and I know that you've never seen me. This is all a huge misunderstanding. If you let me go now, I won't tell anyone, or report it to the police. Just let me out on the street and I can go back to my friend. No one will have to know."

I looked at him, hoping against hope that he would realize his mistake. He would signal to his driver to stop the car, and send me on my way. No one would be the wiser, and I could go back to the bar and drink myself into oblivion forgetting this had ever happened.

But of course, that wasn't how it happened.

"I am telling you the truth. I'm Adrian Masters, your husband. You are my lovely black queen, Anastasia Masters. I am your husband for all eternity," he said with a smirk.

"Why do you call me Anastasia? And I am no one's wife! My name is Anna Jones."

"Short for Anastasia. I won't bare to part any single syllable of it. I have waited with patience and with great purpose. I have now found my one, true love again. I need your love and your tender affections, but I fear that time has taken even that away from me. I won't allow fate to rip you away from me again."

My unwilling gaze honed into Adrian's eyes and I felt compelled to tell him that I do love him, but I am afraid. *Wait, where the hell did that thought come from?* My body shook with terror, I eased my back against the door, as far away as I could get from this maniac. Although Adrian is impressively built with light grey eyes and long dark hair, I'd rather face a hundred muggers like last night than to face this one man alone.

I MUST BE CRAZY. I must have slid into the twilight zone or be living out some horrible nightmare. I closed my eyes tight and wished for a do-over. I wanted to click my booted heels together two times–or maybe ten–and wind back up in my apartment; safe from the kidnappers of this world. In all of my twenty-seven years, I've never been this afraid. I would rather be slaving away at the desk doing mounds of Amanda's work than here.

How long will it take for Cammy to snap out of whatever trance she was in to realize I was gone? Would she call the cops, and have them come after me? Would they even know where to start?

That's how these human trafficking schemes went, I imagined. They were performed seamlessly, in the middle of a crowded bar where no one would pay attention to you, even if I had been kicking and screaming the whole way to the car. People probably just thought I was drunk. It was the perfect crime, I thought. No one wanted to be bothered while someone was being kidnapped right under their noses.

I sat up and tried to look out the windows, but with their dark tint and the time of night, I could barely see anything. We passed by what looked like a row of trees, but I couldn't be sure.

The limo was picking up speed. Where could we possibly be going? It felt like we were leaving the city. I tried to pay attention to every bump and every turn, like I'd seen in the true-crime TV shows that I watched. If I could try and figure out where we were going, then maybe I could find a phone and tell someone where I was, and they could come and find me.

But there weren't any bumps in the road, and we had stopped making turns. We were on some long, dark road that I couldn't make out. We would have to start slowing down eventually, I thought. I looked over to the door handle. I wonder if they're locked on the outside, like in a police car. It would make sense for this woman-snatching vehicle. But if they weren't, maybe I could open it and jump out when they did slow down.

I would probably get hurt, but I would still be able to get up most likely. And then I could start running.

With the adrenaline pumping through me, I could probably run a marathon right now. I'd run as fast as I could, and flag down the next car that came by. There had to be someone else out on this road. And then I could tell them all about this crazy guy and how he had abducted me from the club, right in front of everyone.

I moved closer to the door, trying to see if I could get my hand on the door handle without him noticing. Unfortunately, he was studying my every move intently, just as a predator stalks his prey before he goes in for the kill. Maybe it was just an honest case of mistaken identity. He thought I was his wife, but maybe I just looked really like her doppelganger or something. The more he looked at me, the more he'd realize I wasn't her. At least, I didn't think I was her.

Of course, I wasn't. Wouldn't I remember if I'd marry some tall, charismatic stranger that drove around in a limo? Details like that you don't forget in life. But why did it all seem so foggy? I just pray it will all be sorted soon.

"The doors are locked. You won't be able to escape, Anastasia."

I moved my hand away from the door. How did he know that's what I was going for? It was probably a common move for all the women that he abducted to do. He must've had that feature put in just for that purpose.

"Please let me go. I am not your wife. I am Anna Jones, and I just want to go back to my friend. I don't know you, and I've never met you in my entire life. You have to let me go before this goes any further."

"It is fate that brought us back together. I've been searching for you for over a hundred years," Adrian said, glancing at me.

I looked over at Adrian and cringed even further back against the door. His deep, familiar voice echoed in my ears and summoned a longing from deep within. I tried my best to fight the overwhelming feeling inside. I closed my eyes to block out the noise and images that flooded my memory, but the images emerged like a movie on a reel inside my head...

The late evening sun beat down vengefully on my head. It seemed like I had been running for days on end.

I haven't had barely anything to eat since I left. I put my hand to my stomach and press down, trying to stop the hunger pains that I feel. Knowing that I can't go on like this forever, I stop and pick a few blackberries off a bush near the path. As I shove the berries into my mouth and eat them as quickly as I can, I hear a peculiar sound nearby of rushing water. Grabbing a few more berries and stuffing them in my pocket, I step through the woods to find a small stream with flowing water.

I rush over to the stream and cup my hands, bringing

water to my mouth and soothing my dry, parched throat. I can't stop for long, I know. Once I'd drunk my fill, I sat back and trembled. I hugged my body and stood up, trying to ignore the sheer terror that had overcome me. My body was tired and ready to give up. I had lost so much, and ran for so long, that I began to think of ending it. If I gave myself over now, they would surely kill me. Perhaps that's how this would end for me. I was running and running, but I could only run so far before exhaustion overtook me.

But I knew deep down that stopping now was not a choice I could make. I had to endure and hold on a little longer before I reached my end. Before I would be safe. If they captured me, they would win. I could not let them have that power over me. I may die running from them, but at least I will die from my own hand.

The man who had been my family's slave owner was ruthless, killing my mama, my papa, and my baby brother without a cause. I was the only one left. I did what my papa made me promise I would do if I ever had the chance. I ran — and I ran – and I ran.

I followed the stream into the woods, running through the shallow water to cool my aching feet. They had cuts and scrapes all about them and would need to be looked after if I ever made it out of here. I had to make it out of this place, for Mama and Papa's sake. I could not let their deaths be in vain. I had to make sure that their daughter found her escape from the slave master.

At that moment, I heard voices... lots of them. I stopped and stepped into an overhang of a tree, trying to hide myself as best I could from view. The search party became louder and louder until they were not ten feet from where I hid. I closed my eyes and bit into my shoulder, trying not to make a sound. I could hear them shouting at one another. For a moment, I thought this would be it. They would find me here. I held my breath, counting the seconds until I was called out and seized.

But instead, they rode off down the stream until I could hear them no longer. I caught glimpses of their faces as they rushed by where I was hidden. Some had laterns held high.

They were white men all around the deep forest on horses. Some had a long and thick, black braided whip in hand. I knew they wanted to beat me like they did my family. I had no doubt they wanted to leave my body out to bleed for the scavengers to feast on.

I started running again. I was beyond ravenous, sleep-deprived and lost, but I had to keep in mind I must keep on going if I wanted to live. I didn't know how far I had run. I could no longer hear the dogs barking or the horses' hooves. I'm tired —so tired. My sackcloth dress was in tatters. Maybe I should just give up and die...

"There she is!" Lanterns came into view out of nowhere at the sound of the voice. Before I knew it, men encircled me.

"Oh, God!" I screamed like an injured banshee into the night.

"Hang her!" A harsh voice called out. The rest of the voices loudly agreed in unison. A whip lashed out against my flesh; the pain brought me down to my knees.

"Ow," I screamed in tortured pain. I fell into a tight ball on the damp ground. Strikes on all sides hit my frame. My sobs did nothing to deflect the whips. A feral growl and then a hiss reverberated through the night. The rustle of trees followed the strange sounds. My face remained buried in my hands. Suddenly, someone's tortured scream, unlike any I had heard before, flowed through the air. I continued to sob, finally daring a peek as more screams vibrated across the land. The smell of blood clung in the air. A body fell before me, and I jumped to my feet. I screamed; adding to the screams of the tortured that already hovered through the forest. Suddenly, all was silent except my own sorrowful scream filled with fright. The fallen lanterns and the moon-lighted the night in a shrouded glow. A dark figure of mist appeared before me; his eyes lit up with a face covered in blood.

The world went black before me.

CHAPTER FIVE
ANNA

"ANASTASIA, CAN YOU HEAR ME?" A warm breath ruffled my hair near my left ear. "You remember, don't you? Tell me what you remember."

"I don't remember a damn thing," I lied.

I looked through the fogginess of my mind, trying to find an explanation for what I had just seen. It was almost like the dream I had over and over, but this time it felt more real. I could feel the pain from the whip, and the blood oozing from my torn flesh. I could hear the blood-curdling screams in my ears as I cried out with each lash of the master's whip.

What was happening to me? I looked over at Adrian. Was he some sort of psychologist, or hypnotist, maybe? Was this some sort of mind-altering experiment that I was participating in? Quite unwillingly, I might add. Could he make me see things that weren't really happening, or things that I thought were happening to me? Maybe it was the rum and coke. He must've known the bartender and told him to put something in my drink. That was it. This was all some sort of weird drug-induced hallucination, and I'd snap out of it soon and be back home, safe and sound in no time.

Although, I knew that wasn't the truth. I didn't take any drugs, and this was not some sort of messed-up mind control experiment. Everything that was happening was real, and deep down I knew everything I saw had been real too.

I didn't know why, but everything was so familiar. Running through the woods, eating the berries off a bush and hiding while listening out for the men on their horses. It was all as if I'd done it before. I can remember feeling the terror and the exhaustion, and the indescribable pain as I was whipped. And then the fear I felt as I looked into his eyes. It had all really happened. I could remember it clearly now, as plain as day. But that was impossible. Those events had happened over a hundred and fifty years ago. There was no way that I could've been there.

I hugged my arms around my sides. I wanted to get out of here and go back to my boring, repetitive life. I wanted to go back to Cammy and watch her pick up guys at the bar while I sat there and drank rum and cokes. I wanted to go home and sleep in my bed and not worry about muggers and potential rapists and kidnappers. I just wanted to feel safe again. I moved over to the little window between the back seat and the driver.

"Driver, please take me home," I yelled, but he did nothing; he didn't even turn around. "You both will be arrested," I turned toward Adrian with pleading eyes. "Kidnapping is a federal offense and is punishable by law."

"Do you think I care about your law, Anastasia? I only care about you," Adrian looked deeply into my eyes. I wanted to look away, but something forced me to hold his stare.

"You should care. What did you do to my best friend Cammy? Why did she obey you in the way she did? I–"

I became quiet when his hand cupped my cheek and his other hand threaded through my chin-length, loosely curled hair. I froze when one hand trailed up my neckline and his fingers stroked the pulse that beat at my neck. His eyes flashed a fiery red before his head bent and brought his lips against my own. I gasped, and his tongue plunged into my mouth. His kiss tasted like tart cherries.

No, my mind screamed, but my body had a mind of

its own. My nipples hardened. The atmosphere in the limo grew warm and dense. My mouth opened and closed as I attempted to speak but could not. Adrian's hand splayed at my waist. He suddenly pulled me onto his lap to straddle his waist. My short skirt jacked up high on my thighs, barely covering my ass cheeks.

"My beautiful queen," he muttered low like. His sexy voice caused my nether regions to become slick; my heart hammered incessantly against my chest.

Please let me go, my mind silently cried. My treacherous body failed to obey.

Adrian's kisses consumed me; my bikini panties became saturated with wetness that seeped from my plump slippery folds. His erection pressed against my panty-clad mound. My hips rose and fell in a circular motion. One hand slipped under the crotch of my underwear and his long, graceful fingers gently began to stroke me. His tongue captured my own as he continued to ravage my mouth.

"My beloved," he whispered in repetition against my lips. His voice soothed me the more he spoke. He became less frightening in my thoughts. Tears ebbed and flowed from my eyes. My nipples peaked even harder begging for attention.

"Anastasia, my darling. You have nothing to fear. You belong to me and with me. With you by my side, I can finally claim a true home." Adrian peppered soft kisses all over my face. His slow, rhythmic grinding set my core afire. His hand at my waist assisted my body to move up and down on his growing erection.

I hung on the precipice of pain and pleasure. I closed my eyes, and my head hung limply against my neck. My moans filled the interior of the car. I had no worries about the driver hearing us because Adrian had pressed a button to enclose us in our own space.

Adrian's fingers slid in and out of my slick heat. I wanted more. I needed more. So much so that I cried out, more!

Adrian chuckled and pressed me closer. My body became an inferno. I'm pressing even closer to him and taking delight in riding his massive feeling cock that rested beneath his pants. I gripped each of his shoulders. His rough tongue licked against my neck and a hissing sound vibrated against my throat. I felt a tiny prick followed by the wetness of his tongue. A guttural growl permeated the air. I shuddered and swayed faster against Adrian's crotch.

Suddenly, I spasmed. My orgasm was riveting and made me let loose a prolonged moan. Another guttural growl from Adrian rents the atmosphere and I slumped into Adrian's embrace. Peace settled over me after my sweet release.

Gently, Adrian pushed me away. "Sleep beloved," he touched my face. My body became heavy, and my mind became foggy. I took one look into his eyes before everything went dark, I knew at once that I was forever lost.

CHAPTER SIX
ANNA

I AWOKE in a place unfamiliar to me. I'm in a huge bed covered with a dark burgundy bedspread. I look around the room. Everything is dark; so very dark. I threw the bed covers back and slipped from the bed. My feet met the plushness of a soft rug that covered the entire floor. I wasted no time in flipping the light switch once I found it and noticed a dark mahogany bookcase covered one wall. I walked over to inspect the books that were lined neatly on the shelves. Most appeared to be old, but a few were modern-day books. There are dark burgundy draperies hanging at the windows, and several old-looking paintings hanging from the walls. One picture depicts a woman with dark brown skin. She looks just like me. *But how can that be?* My hair may be different, but the face is the exact same.

"Anastasia, come to me," Adrian's voice echoed in my head. My hand flew to my neck. I walked over to the dresser mirror. I don't know why I inspected my neck, but I did. There are no marks of any kind as far as I can see.

"Anastasia. Come now," the voice says forcefully. My mind has been in such peril. I look down at the lacy white gown I have on and wondered where it came from. I glanced over at the bed where a matching robe was placed. I grabbed it and slid it over my too revealing gown as I walked out of the room.

I gasped, almost stumbling into Adrian's chest.

"Are you all right?" he questions, grabbing me around the waist to keep me from hitting his solid frame.

"No, I'm not okay. I was kidnapped and woke up in a strange place that looks like a dungeon. Why is it so dark in here? I want to go home."

"You can forget about that, my darling. You are at home. I hope you slept well."

Adrian's stare is magnetic. I couldn't help but grow warm all over. "How do you feel?"

"I'm—," my stomach took that moment to growl and I flushed with embarrassment.

"Come. I will feed you. Sometimes I forget," he said. Adrian placed his hand at the small of my back to urge me along.

"Sometimes you forget what?" I asked as we made it to a set of circular stairs. We were halfway down before he spoke again.

"We shall talk after you are fed, Anastasia."

"My name is Anna. Not Anastasia. Please stop calling me that."

"You are Anastasia Masters. Get used to it," he replied in an autoreactive voice.

I bristled from his words but remained quiet. Once we made it down the long circular staircase, he led me into a large dining room. One place setting was laid out and an array of breakfast food was displayed on the table.

"Have a seat," he said as he pulled out a velvet-covered seat for me.

"Aren't you going to eat?" I asked once I became settled.

"No. I've already had my fill," Adrian's gaze brightened, and I had the feeling he was holding some vital piece of information back from me.

"Eat up, my beloved. You will need your strength."

My heart raced against my chest. I felt the push-pull of emotion in his radiant gaze. I grabbed a croissant and slathered it with strawberry jam. I brought the food to my lips and took a bite. Adrian watched me like he was the predator and I was the prey. *Are you trying to fatten me up to kill me?* The words fled through my head.

"No, my darling. I'm not going to kill you. I'm going to make love to you until you remember who you belong to–until you remember I'm your husband and you are my wife. Then I will make it where you will never leave my side again."

My head suddenly began to throb, and my appetite fled as I watched him watching me.

CHAPTER SEVEN
ANNA

"EITHER LET me go home or kill me!" I ordered.

"No. I would never harm you. Don't say such things, my beloved." Adrian stood and walked toward me. I hopped up from the table, backing away, looking around trying to devise my escape. I saw a doorway; I don't know where it leads but I take off in a sprint. In a flash, Adrian is blocking the doorway.

"Wait–, how—how did you do that? You were just back near the dining table," I told him grabbing my head. God! I've surely lost my mind. Tears ebbed from my eyes and flowed down my cheeks. I became weak at the knees and started to fall.

Suddenly, I'm being swept up into Adrian's arms. I close my eyes and become limp. *I give up,* my mind screamed. I feel myself being placed on something soft. I can't bear to open my eyes to investigate my surroundings. Adrian's hand brushes my fluffy hair from my face. I know I must have bedhead, but I don't care. His hand brushes against my cheek and I tremble. *Why does my body always react this way to Adrian?*

"I'm not your wife. Will you please let me go?" I asked Adrian. "I know my friend Cammy must be worried sick about me. She's the only family that I call family left in this world." I finally opened my eyes and hoped my pleas hadn't fallen on deafened ears.

"I am your family. I can't allow you to leave me. I can't go on without you."

"Please, I won't tell anyone that you took me. If you–,"

Adrian didn't allow me to finish my words. "You will see in time that we are meant to be together. It's destiny, my beloved." He swept me into his arms and gazed down at me as if in deep thought. His gaze slid down to my robe. With the flick of a wrist, my robe opened and revealed my body in the lace white gown.

"You look utterly beautiful," he declared. Adrian had blatantly disregarded my plea. My head dropped down in despair.

"Don't look away from me, Anastasia." No other words were needed. I obeyed his command. "Look at who I truly am." For the first time, he smiled, and I noticed his gleaming canine-like teeth. I was up close and personal to a vampire. Instead of being frightened, a sudden calm overcame me like never before. Without thought, I reached out to touch his fangs.

I will never hurt you, Adrian's deep voice echoed in my head. *Close your eyes and remember me. Remember our love and what we meant to each other.* My eyes closed and once again the memories emerged. I did nothing to stop them.

I was running. The laughter of the men who wanted me dead scared me. Suddenly, a man swooped down from the sky like a dark angel to save me. His name was Adrian, and he was a vampire. We knew then and there that we were meant for each other. I became his, and he became mine. He would visit me every night and stay with me until sunrise, making love for hours and hours. But then he would leave me to live out my human life in the sun. I wanted to be near him always. It consumed my every waking thought. I begged Adrian to make me like him so I would never have to feel fear again, but he wouldn't do it. Adrian said he was damned to a life of hell, but he would love me to the very end. Years went by and I got older; my hair grayed and my skin wrinkled. The beauty I had in my youth was beginning to fade away, and Adrian remained forever young. I couldn't stand the thought of getting old and losing him. Every day I would find something that had changed about my body, some new ache or pain that came with old age. Adrian swore to always love me, but I didn't want to put him through the pain of watching me grow old and useless. I couldn't bear it. I wanted to preserve the love we had, and the feeling he had for me as I was. I knew the only path to preservation was to end my life.

One night when Adrian was away, I stole away into the woods, running as fast as my aged legs could take me. I ran until I reached the edge of a steep cliff. I stepped forward slowly, my nightdress billowing around me from the wind. I found myself in the darkest of nights, throwing myself over a cliff. I remember falling and falling into a deep chasm that never seemed to end, and then nothingness.

CHAPTER EIGHT
ANASTASIA

"OH MY GOD!" My eyes flew open.

"Now you remember?" he asked.

"Yes," I sobbed. "Why Adrian? Why did you allow me to grow old? Why did you save me that day if you had to–?"

"Lose you again in death?" he said, finishing my question for me.

"Yes," I nodded as more tears fell down my brown cheeks.

"Never again my beloved. This day I make you mine for all eternity. Fate will never rob you from me again," Adrian's words caused the last vestiges of my uncertainty to dissipate. My soul had been missing something. I never realized what it was until now.

"Yes, I'm ready. Make me yours forever."

I wasn't afraid when Adrian leaned down to mesh his mouth with my own. I could feel the protrusion of his fangs against my lips. Adrian easily stripped me of my robe, gown and panties before removing his own clothing. He was a spectacular specimen to behold, but his cock was huge in length and girth. I opened my arms to him as he came down onto the bed. He stretched out his long muscular frame beside me. Our limbs intertwined, and I buried my hands in the long silken black strands of his hair.

"Mm," I moaned when his lips captured a nipple in his mouth and gave it a gentle suck. Desire flooded through my entire being and nectar began to seep from deep within my heated core. Adrian's erection pulsed heavy against my belly.

My body writhed beneath him as he continued to lave from one nipple to the other. Nothing existed but Adrian and the things he was doing to my body. I craved to feel the rock-solid proof of Adrian's erection inside of me.

"Please, Adrian. Make love to me."

"Tell me what I need to hear," he grunted and ran his tongue over my breasts. "Tell me, Anastasia. My beloved wife."

The throbbing between my thighs intensified. My heart rate increased and my blood boiled through my veins to a feverish point. "I love you, my husband. I'm yours forever and always." My words gave way to his demands most willingly.

"Open wider," Adrian's harsh grunt reached my ears as he pried my thighs further apart. His shaft knocked at my entrance, and I gasped when he started to push inside my core. The pain of his humongous cock prying inside of me soon gave way from the pleasure it provided.

"Oh my yes, Adrian!" I shouted, closing my eyes on a lusty sigh.

He gave another long shove and penetrated me to the hilt. My entire being melted like hot, buttery caramel beneath the pleasure-filled tutelage of my husband.

"Look at me when I'm fucking you," Adrian hissed.

My eyes popped open to take in my beloved's passion-filled face. His eyes were aflame, and his fangs caused electrical shocks to pulse through my wet sex. Adrian slightly withdrew, only to drive himself harder and deeper into me. I welcomed every excruciating, pleasure-filled stroke and dug my nails into the wide expanse of his shoulders. Tears flowed wetting my cheeks, sliding down between our meshing mouths. Adrian pumped into me even harder. I shuddered under his total mastery while his grunts brought me closer to my release.

"Please love me forever, Adrian."

Adrian moaned out my name, suddenly tightening his grasp on me. In a single swift thrust, he impaled me even deeper. I let loose a lusty whine. Hard like steel, Adrian filled me, completely; giving me what no other man could ever give me. He captured my whine with a desirous kiss, repeatedly sliding his thick shaft into my core. I kept my thighs widely spread to fit his every stroke. Intense powerful waves of delight were already overtaking me. My body arched; the twin peaks of my breasts pressed against Adrian's chest. He responded immediately and his hands cupped my ass cheeks to bring us closer together. My eyes opened wider when I felt the slither of his tongue against my neck.

I craned my neck sideways to give him better access to have his way with me. "Bite me, my love. Bite me now," I cried out. My dark angel lifted his face to the ceiling and let out a feral hiss. He then leaned down with his mouth wide open; I felt his fangs against my neck. I arched my back in harmony with his movements, keeping up with his vigorous thrusts.

My destiny was set, and I was ready to meet it head-on with my beloved husband by my side. With no regrets, it happened. The pain when he bit into my flesh was overwhelming. I felt the wetness of my blood sliding down my neck. Agonizing pain racked through my body; mixed with crushing pleasure. An orgasm had me capitulating off a cliff of bliss. Adrian grunted, hissed and growled as his hot seed pulsed and splashed against my inner walls.

His fangs deepened into my flesh and drinking his fill, my flesh gave in to Adrian's piercing canine teeth. The richness of my blood-filled Adrian's mouth. I trembled, trying to gasp for air. Once again, I faded into inky black nothingness of pure bliss.

EPILOGUE
ANASTASIA

ONE HUNDRED YEARS LATER...

We walked along the crowded street, passing by groups of people hustling into the bars and restaurants. It was the weekend, and everyone was out celebrating their lives in some way or another. I smiled at a pair of girlfriends walking into a bar, fixing their hair and smoothing out their dresses as they got ready for a night of drinks and laughs.

All of a sudden, the sky opens up and heavy rain comes down in sheets, forcing everyone on the sidewalk to hurry into the nearest open business. Adrian looked at me. His smooth sexy voice entered my head.

Would you like to go indoors?

I shook my head. I loved the rain, and so I encouraged him to continue along with me. The rain always felt good on my cold skin. I raised my head and closed my eyes, feeling the droplets of water trickle down my face. I opened my eyes and looked over at Adrian. He was smiling at me.

You have always loved the rain. Even in your other lives. If you would like to keep walking, I will stay with you. I'll always stay with you.

I smiled and leaned into him, watching as the rain fell down the front of his expensive coat.

We walked along, watching as cabs drove by looking for stranded passengers. We reached the end of the street.

Where shall we go now, my love?

"The woods. Take me to the woods," I spoke aloud, smiling at the memories the place had held for us.

He nodded and turned down the next street headed towards the woods.

Adrian and I walked hand in hand in the very spot he saved me from centuries ago. The woods were no longer wooded. High-rise buildings, supermarkets, and businesses now littered the area. I no longer felt a void in my life from missing my family. Adrian was my family now. Unbeknownst to me, he had always been.

A single bite from his vampire's kiss has led me to a life of eternity with the man that I loved. No one has ever shown me the type of love that Adrian has bestowed upon me. Not a day goes by that he doesn't tell me and show me the depth of his love for me.

Adrian holds me to his side as we look out over the city.

What do you see, my love?

"Our history. Our lives were spent together in this place. It may continue to change like this," I gestured to the high-rise buildings, "but the land will always be ours. It will always mean something to us. This was the place where we fell in love, where we vowed to live our lives together, and where you made me yours forever. I will always treasure this land, because it brought me to you over multiple lifetimes. I will never stop being grateful for this land."

I can feel the happiness flowing from his pores. We are telepathically connected. Even in my second life when he was a stranger to me, we held that connection. Standing here under the moonlight, I take joy for the time we've had together. Whether it be a day or forever, I'm so happy that Adrian found me again and made me his.

For he is mine and I am his. His Betrothed Wife forever.

THE END

ABOUT THE AUTHOR

Theresa Hodge is an Alabama native-loving mother, sister, aunt, and friend. She is at her best when she is able to bring happiness to others. This author loves to read almost as much as she loves to write fictional stories. She finds writing therapeutic at times, especially during the loss of her oldest sister from breast cancer, which birthed her "Ask Me Again" Series. This was her first but this compilation led to her writing several other books. These books include her bestselling Noelle's Rock series among many others.

Additionally, Theresa has a love affair with poetry. She began writing poetry at an early age and it served as a catalyst for her growth as a writer.

If Theresa can bring a smile to your face and encourage someone else along her journey, she considers it a blessing beyond measure.

KEEP IN TOUCH

TWITTER: (@Poetic__Life): https://twitter.com/Poetic__Life?s=09

Like Page: https://www.facebook.com/askmeagainromanceseries/

Instagram: http://Instagram.com/gemini2goddess

Goodreads: https://www.goodreads.com/author/show/6927856.Theresa_Hodge

BookBub: https://www.bookbub.com/profile/theresa-hodge

Pinterest: https://www.pinterest.com/terehod/

Newsletter Sign-up: http://amazon.us9.list-manage.com/subscribe?u=ffde15be91b185d57d934a65c&id=1f6b614090

Website: https://www.amazon.com/Theresa-Hodge/e/B00J53PB3E

https://terehod.wixsite.com/mysite-1